B·O·O·K

Alexander Dumas's

Monte Cristo's
Prison Years

Retold by

Linda Lott

Illustrated by

Jeremy Jarvis

Columbus, OH

SRAonline.com

 SRA

Send all inquiries to this address:
SRA/McGraw-Hill
4400 Easton Commons
Columbus, OH 43219

Printed in the United States of America.

ISBN: 978-0-07-612189-2
MHID: 0-07-612189-5

5 6 7 8 9 QVS 15 14 13

The McGraw-Hill Companies

Contents

Introduction

The Count of Monte Cristo is the story of Edmond Dantès. This story takes place a long time ago in France. Dantès is a kind, handsome young man. He is about to marry a woman named Mercédès and become the captain of a ship. He is well liked by most people. However, he has four enemies, including one named Villefort. Some of these men are jealous of Dantès. Some fear that what he knows will ruin them.

His enemies plot to frame Dantès for treason. An hour before his wedding to Mercédès, Dantès is arrested. At the jail, Dantès is questioned by the prosecutor, Villefort. Villefort decides Dantès is innocent.

Then Villefort asks to see the letter that caused the problem. It is then Villefort learns his own father is the real traitor. Because he can't let anyone else find out, Villefort burns the letter and promises Dantès he will be freed.

Of course, this is just a trick to get Dantès out of his office. Villefort is really going to send Dantès to prison for the rest of his life. Villefort would be ruined if anyone found out about the letter.

After 14 years in prison, Dantès will escape, become the Count of Monte Cristo, and get even with his enemies.

This part of the story opens as the guards take Dantès to the prison.

Chapter 1

The Prison

In an instant Dantès was placed in a boat between two guards. Soon they were outside the inner harbor.

"Where are you taking me?" Dantès asked.

"We cannot tell you," one of the guards said.

Strange thoughts passed through his mind. The boat they were in could not make a long trip. There was no ship outside the harbor. Perhaps they were going to leave him on some faraway point. He was not chained. They had not tried to handcuff him. This seemed a good sign. Besides, had Villefort not told him he had nothing to be afraid of? Had Dantès not seen Villefort burn the fatal letter? It was the only proof against him.

*Dantès turned and saw they had gone out to sea. He turned to the nearest guard. "Comrade," he said, "I beg you to tell me where we are going. I am Captain Dantès, a loyal Frenchman. Tell me where you are taking me. I promise you on my honor I will accept my fate."

Then a guard asked him, "You are from Marseilles and are a sailor, and yet you do not know where you are going?"

"On my honor, I have no idea."

"Unless you cannot see, or have never been outside the harbor, you must know," the guard said.

"I do not."

"Look around you."

Dantès rose and looked forward. Then he saw the black and frowning rock on which the prison stands.

"The prison?" he cried. "Why* are we going there?"

The guards smiled.

"I am not going there to be jailed," Dantès said. "I have committed no crime. Am I being taken to the prison to be jailed there?"

"It is likely," one of the guards replied.

"Without any questioning?"

"You have been questioned."

"And so, in spite of Villefort's promises?"

"I do not know what Villefort promised you," the guard said. "But I know we are taking you to the prison."

Suddenly Dantès sprang forward to jump into the sea. But four arms grabbed him. He fell back screaming.

For a time the idea of struggling crossed Dantès's mind. But he remembered Villefort's promise.

Then the boat landed. The guards forced him to rise. They dragged him toward the steps that led to the gate of the prison.

Dantès was like a man in a dream. He saw soldiers on the wall. He knew he was going up a flight of steps. He knew he passed through a door. He knew the door closed behind him. But it was like looking through a mist.

They stood for nearly ten minutes. The guards seemed to be waiting for orders. Then the orders came.

"Where is the prisoner?" the jailer asked.

"Here," the guards answered.

"Let him follow me; I will take him to his cell."

"Go!" the guards said, pushing Dantès forward.

The jailer led Dantès into a room almost underground. Its bare and stinking walls seemed soaked with tears. A lamp lit the room faintly.

"Here is your room for tonight," the jailer said. "It is late, and the governor is asleep. Tomorrow, perhaps, he might put you somewhere else. In the meantime there is bread, water, and fresh straw. That is all a prisoner can wish for. Good night." The jailer left with the lamp and closed the door. Dantès was alone in the dark and the cold.

Chapter 2

A Worse Place

In the morning the jailer returned. He had orders to leave Dantès where he was. He found the prisoner in the same spot, as if fixed there. Dantès's eyes were swollen from weeping. He had spent the night standing and without sleep.

The jailer touched Dantès on the shoulder.

"Have you not slept?" the jailer asked.

"I do not know," Dantès answered. The jailer stared at him.

"Are you hungry?" he asked.

"I do not know," Dantès replied.

"Do you wish for anything?"

"I wish to see the governor."

The jailer shrugged his shoulders. "What you ask is impossible. But if you are very well behaved, you will be allowed to walk about. Someday you will meet the governor, and he might talk to you."

"But," Dantès said, "how long shall I have to wait?"

"Ah, a month—six months—a year."

"It is too long a time. I wish to see him at once."

"Ah," the jailer said, "do not always think about the impossible, or you will be mad in two weeks."

"You think so?"

"Yes. The abbot who was in this cell before you went mad. He offered the government a million francs for his freedom."

"How long since he left the cell?"

"Two years."

*"Was he set free, then?"

"No. He was put in a dungeon."

"Listen!" Dantès said. "I am not an abbot. I am not mad. Perhaps I shall be, but for now, I am not. I will make you another offer."

"What is that?"

"I do not offer you a million francs because I do not have it. I will give you 100 francs. The first time you go to Marseilles, you must find a young girl named Mercédès and give her a note from me."

"If I took the francs and were discovered, I would lose my job, which is worth 2,000 francs a year. I would be a great fool to run such a risk for only 100."

"Well," Dantès said, "remember this. I will someday hide myself behind* the door, and when you enter I will hit you with this stool."

"Threats!" the jailer cried. "You are going mad. The abbot began like you. In three days you will be mad like him. Luckily, there are dungeons here."

Dantès whirled the stool round his head.

"All right, all right," the jailer said. "I will send word to the governor."

"Very well," Dantès said, dropping the stool.

The jailer went out and returned with five soldiers.

"By the governor's orders," he said, "take the prisoner to the floor below."

"To the dungeon, then," a soldier said.

"Yes. We must put the madman with the madmen," the jailer said. The soldiers grabbed Dantès, who went quietly.

They went down 15 steps. The door of a dungeon was opened, and Dantès was pushed in. The door closed. Dantès moved forward until he touched the wall. Then he sat down in the corner until his eyes became used to the darkness. The jailer was right. Dantès was very nearly mad.

—— Chapter 3 ——

The Two Prisoners

Nearly a year and a half later, the inspector of prisons made a visit to the prison. He visited the cells and dungeons of many of the prisoners. He asked how they were fed and whether they had any needs. They all answered that the food was terrible and that they wanted to be set free.

"I do not know why I have to make these useless visits," the inspector said. "When you see one prisoner, you see all. Always the same thing, ill-fed and innocent. Are there any others?"

"Yes. The mad prisoners are in the dungeons," the governor said.

"Let us visit them," the inspector said. "We must play this joke to the end. Let us see the dungeons."

"Let us first send for two soldiers. The prisoners down there are sometimes violent."

Two soldiers were sent for. The inspector moved down a stinking, damp, dark stairway.

"Oh," he cried, "who can live here?"

"A most dangerous traitor. We are ordered to keep a strict watch over him. He is daring and stubborn," the governor said.

"He is alone?"

"Yes."

"How long has he been here?"

"Nearly a year and a half. We have an abbot in another dungeon. He has been here since 1811, and in 1813 he went mad. You had better see him."

"I will see them both," the inspector said. "Let us visit this one first."

"By all means," the governor said. He motioned to a guard to open the door.

Dantès sat in a corner of the dungeon. He raised his head. Then he sprang forward with clasped hands.

"I want to know what crime I have committed. I want to be tried. If I am guilty, I want to be shot. If I am innocent, I want to be set free."

"Are you well fed?" the inspector asked.

"I believe so. I do not know. It does not matter. What matters is that an innocent man has to die in prison."

"You are very mild today," the governor said.

"Being in prison has quieted me. I have been here so long."

"So long? When were you arrested, then?" the inspector asked.

"The 28th of February, 1815, at half past two in the afternoon."

"Today is the 30th of July, 1816. Why, it is but 17 months."

"Only 17 months," Dantès answered. "Oh, you do not know what 17 months is like in prison! I ask only for a trial. Surely you must do that!"

"We shall see," the inspector said.

"Oh, I am free. Then I am saved!"

"Who arrested you?"

"Villefort. See him, and hear what he says."

"Villefort is no longer at Marseilles. He is now at Toulouse," the inspector said.

"I am not surprised," Dantès whispered. "My only help is gone."

"Did Villefort hate you?"

"Oh, no. He was very kind to me."

"I can, then, count on the notes he has left about you?"

"Yes."

"That is well," the inspector said. Then he closed the door of Dantès cell.

"Will you see the records," the governor asked, "or go to the other cells?"

"Let us visit all the cells now," the inspector said. "Once I go up the stairs, I will not have the courage to come down again."

"This next prisoner has the madness," the governor said. "He thinks he has a huge treasure. The first year he offered the government a million francs to be set free. The second, two million; the third, three million; and so on. He is now in his fifth year in prison. He will ask to speak to you and will offer you five million."

"How strange! What is his name?"

"The Abbot Faria. Here he is. Number 27," the governor said.

*In the center of the cell sat a man whose tattered clothes barely covered him.

"What is it you want?" the inspector asked.

"I, sir?" Faria replied. "I want nothing."

"You do not understand," the inspector continued. "I am sent here by the government to visit the prisoners and hear what they need."

"Oh, that is different!" Faria cried. "And we shall understand each other, I hope. I wish to tell you about an important treasure. The government may have it all."

"My dear sir, the government is rich and does not want your treasures," the inspector said. "Keep them until you are freed."

Faria's eyes flashed. He grabbed the inspector's hand. "But what if I am not freed?" he cried. "This treasure will be lost. I will offer six* million. Just give me my freedom."

"On my word," the inspector said in a low tone, "had I not been told this man was mad, I would believe what he says."

"I am not mad," Faria said. "There is a treasure. I offer to sign an agreement with you. I promise to lead you to the spot where you shall dig. If I am not telling the truth, return me to prison."

"Are you well fed?" the inspector asked.

"Promise me," Faria answered. "Free me if what I tell you is true."

"Are you well fed?" the inspector asked again.

"Sir, you run no risk. I will stay here. There is no chance of my escaping."

"You do not answer my question," the inspector said.

"Nor you mine," Faria cried. "You will not accept my gold. I will keep it for myself. "

Later, the inspector kept his word with Dantès. He examined the records and found the following note:

Edmond Dantès:

Violent traitor.

Use the greatest care.

In his report about Dantès, the inspector wrote, "Nothing to be done."

At the end of a year the governor was moved. A new governor arrived. It would have been hard for him to learn the names of the prisoners. So he learned their numbers instead. The unhappy young man was no longer Edmond Dantès. He was now Number 34.

Chapter 4

Number 34 and Number 27

Nearly four years passed. At the end of the second, Dantès had stopped marking time.

"I wish to die," Dantès said. He decided to starve himself. "When my morning and evening meals are brought," he thought, "I will cast them out the window. They will think I have eaten them."

He kept his word. Twice a day he threw out his food. He did this until he did not have enough strength to rise. The next morning he could not see or hear. The jailer feared he was ill. Dantès hoped he was dying.

About nine o'clock in the evening, Dantès heard a sound in the wall against which he was lying.

*He raised his head and listened. It was a continual scratching. The sound lasted nearly three hours. Then Dantès heard the noise of something falling. At last, all was silent.

Hours later the scratching began again. Suddenly the jailer entered Dantès's cell.

The jailer had brought him his breakfast. Dantès began to talk about everything. He had to keep the jailer from hearing the scratching.

The jailer placed the food on the table and left. Dantès listened again. The sound became clearer.

"There can be no doubt about it," he thought. "It is some prisoner trying to dig out. Oh, if only I were there to help him!"

Then he said to himself, "If it is a prisoner, the noise I make will alarm him. He will stop and not* begin again until he thinks everyone is asleep."

Dantès went to a corner of his cell. He removed a stone and knocked it against the wall where he heard the sound. He struck three times. At the first blow the sound stopped.

Dantès listened. An hour passed. Two hours passed. No sound was heard from the wall.

The day passed away in silence. The night passed in silence too. Dantès did not close his eyes.

Three days passed. One evening Dantès heard a faint movement. Someone was at work on the other side of the wall.

Dantès decided he had to help the other prisoner. He began by moving his bed. He tried to find something to use to remove a stone. He saw nothing. There was only one thing Dantès could do. He dropped a jug, and it broke into pieces.

Dantès hid the sharpest pieces in his bed. He could not do much in the night because of the darkness. So he pushed his bed back and waited for day.

All night he heard the workman. After the jailer brought his food in the morning, Dantès moved his bed again. He saw that his work had been useless. He had been attacking the stone instead of the plaster around it.

Dantès began to work. Because the plaster was damp, Dantès could break it off in small pieces. But at this rate, it would take him two years to dig a passage.

Then Dantès had an idea. The jailer always brought Dantès's soup in an iron pan. The handle of this pan was iron too. Dantès would have given ten years of his life for it.

That evening Dantès tricked the jailer into leaving the pan. Dantès quickly ate his food, then he moved his bed. He put the handle of the pan between two stones of the wall and used it as a lever. At the end of an hour, a stone was out of the wall. It left a hole a foot and a half across.

Dantès collected the plaster. He carried it into the corner of his cell and covered it with earth. Then he continued to work. In the morning he put the stone back. He pushed his bed against the wall and lay down.

After Dantès had been working for several nights, he hit something. He touched it and found it was a beam. This beam crossed the hole Dantès had made. He had to dig above or under it.

"Is there no hope?" Dantès whispered. "Do not let this be!"

"Who talks of lost hope?" a voice asked. It seemed to come from the earth. Dantès's hair stood on end. He rose to his knees.

"Speak again," Dantès cried. "Who are you?"

"Who are you?" the voice asked.

"An unhappy prisoner," Dantès answered.

"Of what country?"

"France."

"Your name?"

"Edmond Dantès."

"Your job?"

"A sailor."

"How long have you been here?"

"Since the 28th of February, 1815."

"Your crime?"

"I am innocent."

"But with what were you charged?"

"Of having plotted to help Napoleon return. How long have you been here?" Dantès asked.

"Since 1811. Do not dig anymore," the voice said. "Only tell me, how high up is the hole?"

"On a level with the floor."

"How is it hidden?"

"Behind my bed."

"Has your bed been moved since you have been a prisoner?"

"No."

"What does your cell open on?"

"A hallway."

"And the hallway?"

"On a court."

"I have made a mistake," the voice said. "I took a wrong turn. I thought the wall you are mining was the outer wall of the prison."

"But then you would be close to the sea."

"That is what I had hoped. I would have thrown myself into the sea and swum to one of the islands near here. Then I would have been safe."

"Could you have swum so far?"

"Yes. Stop up the hole carefully. Do not work anymore until you hear from me."

"At least tell me who you are."

"I am . . . I am Number 27."

"You do not trust me, then," Dantès said.

"How old are you? Your voice is that of a young man."

"I do not know my age. I have not counted the years I have been here. All I know is I was just 19 when I was arrested on the 28th of February, 1815."

"Not quite 26!" the voice whispered. "At that age you cannot be a traitor."

"Oh, no, no," Dantès cried. "I would never betray you."

"You have done well to speak to me. I was about to form another plan. I will not forget you. Wait."

"How long?"

"I must figure out our chances. I will give you a signal."

"But you will not leave me. You will come to me, or you will let me come to you. We will escape. If we cannot escape, we will talk," Dantès said.

"We will talk tomorrow," the voice said.

The next morning, as Dantès removed his bed from the wall, he heard three knocks.

"Is it you?" he asked. "I am here."

"Is your jailer gone?" the voice replied.

"Yes," Dantès said. "He will not return until evening. We have 12 hours before us."

"I can work, then?" the voice asked.

"Oh, yes, yes. This instant, I beg you."

In time, part of the floor gave way. From the bottom of the hole, Dantès saw first the head, then the shoulders, and lastly the body of a man, who sprang lightly into his cell.

Chapter 5

The Treasure

For eight years Dantès and the other prisoner, Faria, meet in secret. During this time they plan their escape. Faria also uses this time to teach Dantès history, science, psychology, and several languages.

During their talks, Faria helps Dantès figure out why he is in prison and who is to blame. After Faria becomes ill, he cannot carry out the escape. He tells Dantès he must go on without him. Dantès refuses to leave his friend. Because Dantès has been a true and loyal friend, Faria decides to tell him about the treasure hidden on the Island of Monte Cristo and how to find it. The treasure had belonged to the Spada family.

*This treasure has no owner in the world?" Dantès asked.

"No, no, be easy on that score. The family is dead. The last Count of Spada made me his heir. If we lay hands on this treasure, we may enjoy it without guilt."

"And you say this treasure is worth . . . ?"

"Two million Roman crowns, nearly 13 million francs."

"Impossible!" Dantès said.

"Impossible? And why?" Faria asked. "The Spada family was one of the oldest and most powerful families."

Dantès thought he was in a dream.

"I have only kept this secret so long from you," Faria continued, "so that I might test you and then surprise you. Had we escaped before my illness, I would have taken you to Monte Cristo. Now it is you who will take me there.* Well, Dantès, do you not thank me?"

"This treasure belongs to you, my dear friend, and to you only. I have no right to it. I am not your son."

"You are my son, Dantès," Faria said. "You are the child of my prison years."

—— Chapter 6 ——

Escape

One night Dantès woke up suddenly. He thought someone was calling him. He opened his eyes upon utter darkness. The call came from Faria's cell. "Can it be?" Dantès whispered.

He moved his bed. Then he drew up the stone and rushed into the passage. When he reached the other end, the secret entrance was open. Dantès saw the old man clinging to the bed.

"My dear friend," Faria said, "you understand. I need not tell you."

Dantès uttered a cry. He rushed toward the door, yelling, "Help, help!" Faria had just enough strength to stop him.

"Silence," Faria said, "or you are lost. We must now think only of you, my dear friend."

*Dantès could only clasp his hands and cry, "Oh, my friend, my friend, do not speak this way!"

"There is no hope," Faria replied, shaking his head. "Now lift me onto my bed, for I can no longer support myself."

Dantès took the old man in his arms and placed him on the bed.

"And now, my dear friend," Faria said, "I wish you happiness and riches." The young man fell on his knees, leaning his head against the old man's bed.

"Listen, now, to what I say," Faria said. "There really is a treasure. If you do escape, remember that the poor abbot, whom all the world called mad, was not so. Hurry to Monte Cristo. Find the treasure, for you have suffered long enough." A violent fit attacked* the old man.

"Good-bye," he whispered, clasping Dantès's hand. "Good-bye!"

"Oh, no, no, not yet," Dantès cried. "Do not leave me! Help! Help! Help!"

"Hush, hush!" the dying man whispered. Raising himself, he said, "Monte Cristo, forget not Monte Cristo!" Then he fell back.

Half an hour, an hour, an hour and a half went by. Dantès leaned over his friend. He felt the body grow cold. The heart's beat became deeper and duller until finally it stopped. It was six o'clock in the morning.

Dantès put out the lamp and hid it. Then he went away, closing as well as he could the entrance to the secret passage.

It was time; the jailer was coming. He began his rounds at Dantès's cell, then he went on to Faria's.

Dantès wanted to know what was going on in the dungeon of his friend. He sneaked through the passage and arrived in time to hear a guard call out for help. Other guards came. Last of all came the governor.

Dantès heard the creaking of the bed as they moved the body. He heard them send for the doctor. It seemed to him as if everyone had left the cell. Still, he did not dare to enter, as they might have left a guard to watch the body. He remained in the tunnel, hardly breathing.

At the end of an hour he heard a faint noise, which grew louder. It was the governor returning, followed by the doctor and others. There was silence. The doctor was examining the dead body.

"You may make your mind easy," the doctor said. "He is dead. I will answer for that. I hope you will treat him properly."

"Yes, yes. He shall be buried in the newest sack we can find. Will that do?" the governor asked.

Other footsteps, going and coming, were heard. Then the noise of rustling canvas reached Dantès's ears.

The bed creaked. The heavy footfall of a man lifting a weight sounded on the floor. Then the bed creaked again under the weight dropped on it.

"This evening," the governor said.

Meanwhile, the men put the body in the sack.

"This evening," the governor said again, when the task was ended.

"At what hour?" a guard asked.

"About ten or 11 o'clock."

"Shall we watch the body?"

"Of what use would it be? Shut the dungeon as if he were alive." Then the voices died away. Dantès raised the stone and looked carefully around the cell. It was empty. Dantès came out of the tunnel.

He lifted his hand to his head, feeling as if he were going mad.

"Where does this thought come from?" he asked himself. "None but the dead leave this dungeon. Let me take the place of the dead!"

Without giving himself time to think, he bent over the sack and ripped it open. He took the body from the sack and carried it through the tunnel to his own cell. He laid it on his bed and covered it with his blanket. He kissed the old man. Then he turned Faria's head toward the wall so the jailer might believe he was asleep.

Dantès entered the tunnel again. He pulled his bed against the wall. He returned to the other cell and took from a hiding place a needle and some thread. He got inside the sack, then he sewed up the mouth of the sack from the inside.

If the grave diggers took him to the grave, he would allow himself to be covered with earth. Then he would work his way through the earth and escape.

Footsteps were heard on the stairs. Dantès felt the time had arrived. He held his breath. The footsteps stopped at the door. Then the door opened. A dim light reached Dantès's eyes through the rough sack that covered him. He saw two shadows come to the bed. A third remained at the door. The two men lifted the sack.

"He's heavy for an old, thin man," one man said, as he raised Dantès's head.

"They say every year adds half a pound to the weight of the bones," the other man said.

"Have you tied the knot?" the first man asked.

"What would be the use of carrying so much more weight?" the other man answered. "I can do that when we get there."

"What's the knot for?" Dantès wondered.

They placed Dantès's body on a bier. Dantès stiffened himself like a dead man.

Suddenly he felt the fresh and sharp night air. The men went on for 20 paces and then stopped. One of them went away.

"Give us a light," one man said. "I shall never find what I am looking for."

"What can he be looking for?" Dantès thought. "The spade, perhaps."

"Here it is at last," the other man said.

As he said this, one of the men came toward Dantès, who heard something metal laid down beside him. At the same time a cord was fastened round his feet with a sudden and painful jerk.

"Well, have you tied the knot?" one of the men asked.

"Yes, and pretty tight too."

"Move on, then." The body was lifted once more, and they went on.

They went 50 paces farther, and then stopped to open a door. They went forward again. The noise of the waves smashing against the rocks reached Dantès's ears.

"Bad weather!" one man said. "Not a good night for a dip in the sea."

"Well, here we are at last," the other man said.

"A little farther. You know the last one was stopped on his way by the rocks," the first man said.

They went down five or six more steps. Then Dantès felt them take him, one by the head and the other by the heels, and swing him to and fro. "One! Two! Three!" they said. At that instant, Dantès felt himself flung into the air.

Dantès had been flung into the sea and was dragged into the deep by a 36-pound weight tied to his feet.